The Origami Master

Nathaniel
Lachenmeyer

Illustrated by
Aki Sogabe

www.av2books.com

Your AV² Media Enhanced book gives you a fiction readalong online. Log on to www.av2books.com and enter the unique book code from this page to use your readalong.

AV² Readalong Navigation

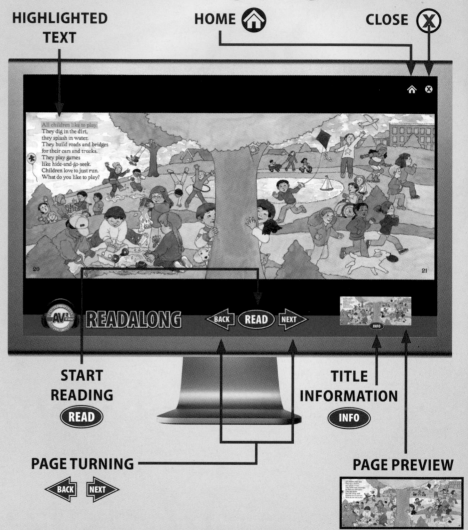

HIGHLIGHTED TEXT

HOME 🏠

CLOSE ❌

START READING READ

PAGE TURNING BACK NEXT

TITLE INFORMATION INFO

PAGE PREVIEW

Go to **www.av2books.com**, and enter this book's unique code.

BOOK CODE

M650977

AV² by Weigl brings you media enhanced books that support active learning.

First Published by

ALBERT WHITMAN & COMPANY
Publishing children's books since 1919

Published by AV² by Weigl
350 5ᵗʰ Avenue, 59ᵗʰ Floor New York, NY 10118
Website: www.av2books.com   www.weigl.com

Library of Congress Control Number: 2013939936

ISBN 978-1-62127-897-9 (hardcover)
ISBN 978-1-48961-455-1 (single-user eBook)
ISBN 978-1-48961-456-8 (multi-user eBook)

Printed in the United States of America in North Mankato, Minnesota
1 2 3 4 5 6 7 8 9 0   17 16 15 14 13

052013
WEP250413

Text copyright ©2008 by Nathaniel Lachenmeyer.
Illustrations copyright ©2008 by Aki Sogabe.
Published in 2008 by Albert Whitman & Company.

The Origami Master

4

$\mathcal{S}$hima the Origami Master lived alone, high up in the mountains. He never had visitors. His origami kept him company.

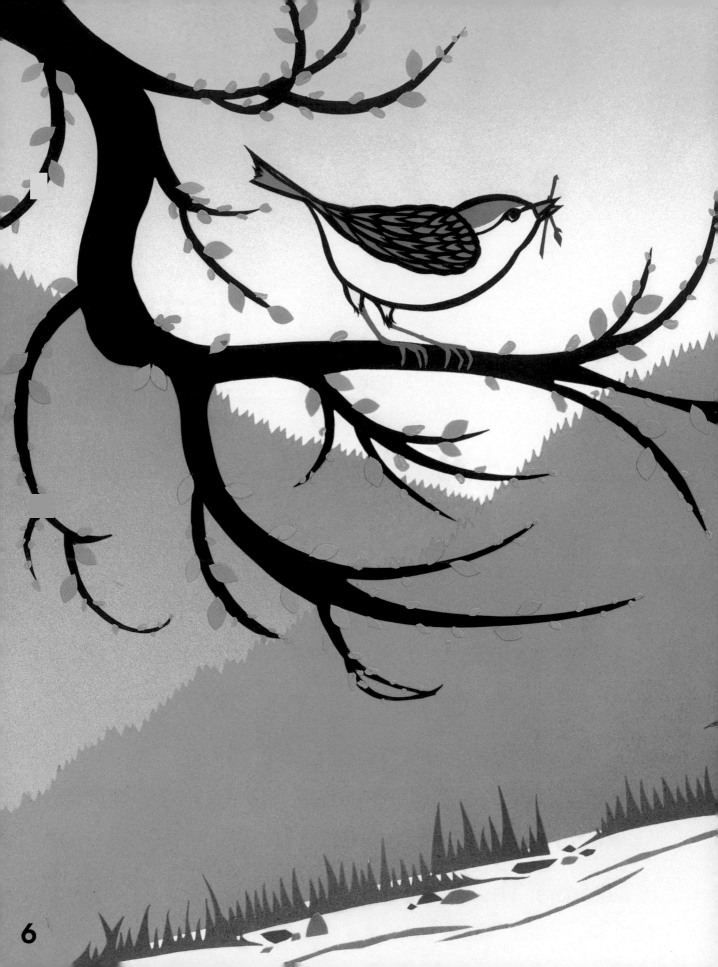

One day, a warbler chose the tree
in Shima's backyard for its nest. It flew
back and forth, collecting twigs.

When the warbler was done for the day, it sat on a branch and watched Shima doing origami. From time to time, it sang: "Hoohokekyo . . . hoohokekyo."

That evening, after Shima went to bed,
the warbler flew in through the open doorway
and alighted on his desk. It began to fold a
piece of paper the way it had seen Shima do.

The next morning, Shima discovered a new paper elephant on his desk. He picked it up and examined it closely. It was simpler and more beautiful than any of the ones he had made. Someone is playing a trick on me, he thought.

Shima threw his elephants away. He decided to make a dragon. In his opinion, his origami dragons were the best in the world.

In the morning, Shima found a magnificent new dragon on his desk. It looked like it was about to come to life and fly back to its lair.

Shima spent the day folding
origami spiders. At dusk, he left his best spider
on his desk. Then, he hid in the hall. He was
determined to find out who was making the origami.

16

In the middle of the night, the warbler flew inside and began making an origami spider. Shima watched in amazement. He decided to try to catch the warbler and learn its secrets.

Just after sunrise, Shima hiked
down the mountain to the city below.

He bought a large birdcage
and a lock, and returned home.

That night, Shima hid under his desk.
When the warbler arrived, he caught it and
put it in the cage.

The warbler cried and beat its wings
against the cage, but it could not escape.

Shima brought the warbler his best origami paper. He gathered nuts and berries for it to eat.

But the warbler just
stared sadly at the tree,
where its nest was waiting.

Shima stayed up all night, making every origami animal he could think of. The warbler did not look at any of them. Finally, as the sun rose in the sky, Shima fell asleep.

When Shima woke up, he found the cage door
open and the warbler gone. The lock was lying
next to the cage. Beside it was an origami key.

Shima ran outside. The warbler's nest was empty. It made Shima sad to think that he had scared the bird away. Then, he saw the warbler returning to the tree with a twig in its beak. He smiled when he heard its beautiful song: "Hoohokekyo . . . hoohokekyo."

29

Shima realized how much he would miss
the warbler if it left. He sat down and began
work on something new—an origami nest for
the friend he had made and almost lost.